JUNE IS FOR JENSEN
MOUNTAIN MEN OF MUSTANG MOUNTAIN

KACI ROSE

Copyright © 2023, by Kaci Rose, Five Little Roses Publishing. All Rights Reserved.

No part of this publication may be reproduced, distributed, or transmitted in any form or by any means, including photocopying, recording, or other electronic or mechanical methods, or by any information storage and retrieval system without the prior written permission of the publisher, except in the case of very brief quotations embodied in critical reviews and certain other noncommercial uses permitted by copyright law.

Publisher's Note: This is a work of fiction. Names, characters, places, and incidents are a product of the author's imagination. Locales and public names are sometimes used for atmospheric purposes. Any resemblance to actual people, living or dead, or to businesses, companies, events, institutions, or locales is completely coincidental.

Book Cover By: Kelly Lambert-Greer

Editing By: Debbe @ **On The Page, Author and PA Services**

To the Match of the Month Patrons, especially...

Jackie Ziegler

And to our supporters on Kickstarter, especially...

Stephanie Scarim

Thank you so much for your support. We couldn't do what we love without you!

CHAPTER 1
JENSEN

I NORMALLY ENJOY Sunday night dinners at Aunt Ruby's house. She's a damn good cook and besides my twin brother Jonas, she and Uncle Orville are the closest family I have. Usually, there's good food and dessert, even if we have to deal with a little of Aunt Ruby's gossip and some talk about how we need to find nice girls.

That talk has been coming up more and more as my MC brothers have been finding love, and Aunt Ruby is really laying it on thick tonight. The reason she's harping on us to find nice girls and settle down becomes painfully clear when I get a text from Luna.

>Luna: Have you seen this?

That's all her text says, but there's a link to the Mustang Mountain tourism website that my aunt runs.

As I click the link, I get a sinking feeling in my stomach.

Jonas and I went to school with Jackson, Ford, and Luna. We were a grade behind Ford and Luna, so it wasn't really until we became adults that we all reconnected. But they've become a second family to us. So, I know for her to reach out, it must be big.

When the page loads, I jump out of my seat, and in a few long strides, I'm in the kitchen where my aunt is cleaning up dishes from dinner.

"What the hell is this, Aunt Ruby?" I ask, showing her the page where she has me listed as Mustang Mountain's Mountain Man of the Month for June.

"Boy, you better watch your mouth! Adult or not, I'll still pop you upside the head with a frozen steak if you cuss like that in my house again." Aunt Ruby turns around to glare at me. Then she glances at the website and shrugs her shoulders. "If you expect me to be any kind of grandparent figure to any kids you might have, it's about time you and your brother settles down. You'd better get going. Your Uncle Orville and I aren't getting any younger."

Jonas walks into the kitchen laughing hysterically. "I knew you were going to be June. I just knew it."

"You'd better shut your mouth because your name starts with a J, and I'd bet anything that she's got you set up to be July." That seems to sober him up pretty quickly as he looks over at Aunt Ruby.

"She wouldn't dare," he says, as if Aunt Ruby isn't standing in the room.

"I would dare. Now get your butt in gear and help me with these dishes," she says, handing the sponge in her hand to Jonas just as my phone starts to ring.

Aunt Ruby glares at me, but I hold up my phone. "It's Courtney," is all I have to say, and Aunt Ruby nods.

She approves of Courtney and me working together to help the women's shelter. I've been the main point of contact when Courtney needs help from my MC brothers, so I get random calls from her at odd times.

"Hey, Courtney," I say, answering the phone.

"Jensen, I require your help. I've got a woman who called, and she and her daughter need to get out of a very unsafe situation tonight. I need backup."

"You've got it. Should I meet you at the normal spot?"

"I'm already on my way there. The sooner you can get there, the better. This one's not pretty," she says, and my blood goes cold. Generally, when Courtney says something like that, it means there are kids involved.

Some of the situations Courtney has helped women out of are things straight out of your worst nightmare's nightmare. Things your brain can't comprehend.

Without even bothering to say goodbye, we just hang up. Every second counts.

"Jonas, we've got to go now. Courtney needs our

help with a really bad case," I tell him, and he drops what he's doing.

"Damn it, we have the bikes," he says.

If we're using our motorcycles, it will make it impossible to make phone calls to the rest of the guys while we're on our way.

"Who do you need me to call?" Aunt Ruby asks.

"Ace and Shaw. Why don't we let the married guys have a peaceful night on this one," I tell her.

She nods, already pulling out her phone.

We each give her a kiss on the cheek and then rush out the door.

Our meeting spot is at the base of the mountain. Ace and Shaw beat us there by a minute or two. I can see the tension on Courtney's face.

We don't waste time with hellos. Instead, she nods, and we follow her down the road. She's driving the women's shelters pickup, a vehicle I insisted on when I found out she was doing pickups in her personal car.

After I made an issue about how unsafe it was for people around town to know her vehicle, she agreed to use the pickup I provided. So now, she has a vehicle specifically for these types of rescues for the women's shelter.

The four of us ride behind her on our bikes. Now that the weather is warm, we're going to get them out as much as we can. Plus, they make for pretty quick getaway vehicles if we need to provide a distraction for her, which we've had to do many times.

All my brothers in the MC club know exactly what

to do. We've all helped on these runs. Honestly, it's really part of why we built our MC club.

We arrive at an old, rundown house that doesn't look like it would be habitable for a human being. The only sign of life is a child's tricycle overturned on the overgrown grass in front of the house.

The place is closer to Whitefish than Mustang Mountain. Distance doesn't matter as we've traveled several hours to help someone in need before.

No sooner do I turn off my bike and get off to walk up with Courtney than a woman steps out of the house. The other men stay on their bikes in case they need to use them to help protect Courtney and me, or block someone from entering or leaving the house.

"Hurry, he's going to be back anytime now. He just got out of work early." Her frightened voice tells me she wasn't expecting the man back so soon.

When she steps into the yard, I can see the woman has a toddler on her hip. Thankfully, the vehicle Courtney uses has car seats in it. Courtney helps the woman get her daughter secured as I grab the bags sitting by the front door.

As expected, there are only three bags. These women usually leave with very little. Some of them don't even go with anything at all.

I grab all three bags and toss them in the back of the truck Courtney's driving.

"Alright, let's go," Courtney says as the woman gets into the car. We waste no time getting Courtney back down the road and making sure she's not followed.

Until we get to the main road and head back towards Mustang Mountain, we don't pass another car. My job is to stay with Courtney if she needs anything. The other guys are making sure that we're not followed. Thankfully, tonight seems to be a pretty easy ride as we get back to the spot where we met up with Courtney earlier tonight.

This is where we part ways with the guys. We don't want to overwhelm the woman, who more than likely would be terrified of four hulking tattooed bikers surrounding her. Not to mention that the rest of the guys have never been to the women's shelter. We keep the location under lock and key, so it's difficult to find on top of all the security measures I've made sure they have in place.

I'm the only guy from the Mustang Mountain Riders that has actually been to the shelter outside of my brother Jonas. Once the other guys are gone, I follow Courtney the rest of the way to the shelter. There's a locked gate at the road as we turn onto the driveway. The entire area is fenced in, along with the security measures that I've set up, including cameras.

It's a mile-long driveway, so even if there was no gate, someone still wouldn't be able to see the place from the road. Plus, the land backs up to a mountain, so it's pretty secure.

Once Courtney parks the vehicle, one of the other women that work at the intake part of the shelter steps out. While I stand back, Courtney takes a few minutes to explain the process to the woman. When the woman who we just rescued hesitantly steps away from the truck, she looks over at me, and gives me a shy, shaky smile.

It's then I get a good look at her and the bruises that cover her body. She has a black eye, a split lip, and blood at the hairline near her temple. Distinct bruises in the shape of handprints fill the arm that's holding her daughter, and her daughter has a fresh bruise on her arm as well.

Her little girl looks to be in much better shape than she is. My guess is her last straw was when the guy put his hands on her daughter. Usually, the women are more than fine taking the beatings themselves, but when their kids are brought into the mix, that's where they draw the line. I hate that it has to get that far before they'll call for help, but I'm glad they call, regardless.

Once the woman is safely inside, Courtney turns back to me. I get off the bike, set my helmet on the handlebars, and walk over to her before pulling her into my arms.

"Thank you for tonight," she says.

Before she goes inside, I know Courtney will sit out here for a few minutes and process what happened. She also knows that I won't leave until she is safely inside because I know she'll be spending the night here.

"I'm here anytime you need me, Courtney. You know that," I say, holding her a bit tighter.

It's moments like this that make me wonder why

Jonas ever broke up with her. I hate they dated in high school in the first place, making her off-limits to me.

"I know, but I still really appreciate it. I'm going to need a day or two to make sure she gets settled in, but we still need to get together to talk about the outing we have planned for the women and kids here."

There's a medieval festival a few towns over. She really wants to take the women and children out for the day to let the kids relax and be kids. But for the women to feel safe enough to go, they'll need support, and they'll need protection.

That means all the Mustang Mountain Riders will be there, even the elders. The club voted to make this outing one of the mandatory events all the guys need to attend. It's not like we could put up a signup form asking for volunteers without bringing attention to the women's shelter and the people we've been protecting.

I'll take any time I can with her because even if she's off-limits, it hasn't stopped me from wanting her.

CHAPTER 2
COURTNEY

I'M MEETING Jensen today for lunch to plan this outing for the women and their kids at the shelter. Like all of our lunch meetings, we're gathering at the cafe in town. The aroma of coffee and baked goods hits me before I walk in the door. Since I'm there first, I grab a booth towards the back, so we'll be out of everyone's way.

From my seat, I can see the menu behind the counter. The specials and drinks are written in black marker on large white boards. The small tables are mostly empty, but I know they'll fill soon enough.

There's only one other table in the place and the couple there are talking quietly with their kids.

I know he's here even before he walks through the door, because I can hear the loud rumble of his motorcycle as he parks on the street in front of the café. Over the years, I've learned the sound of his bike and how to differentiate it from his MC brothers. When you are in my line of work, the details are important.

A moment later, he walks in and I watch his eyes scan the café. He already knows I'm here as my car is parked right out front. When he finally sees me, he smiles and heads my way.

I take a minute to watch and appreciate his large muscular body as he walks over to me in long confident strides. The tight jeans and the leather MC jacket look good on him. Not for the first time I notice how attractive he is, but as always, I dismiss it. These are thoughts I shouldn't be having about my ex-boyfriend's twin brother.

"Have you been here long?" Jensen asks. Then, checking his watch and seeing that he's early, he slides into the booth.

"About fifteen minutes. I had to come into town for something anyway and figured that I'd just hang out here. No point in going back to the shelter just to turn around and come back out," I tell him, shrugging my shoulder. It's mostly true.

The other part of the truth is that I wanted to make sure I got here early enough so that I could watch him walk in like he just did. It's the little pleasures that I allow myself.

"Did you see that Ruby is still at it?" He says as we wait for the server.

"Oh, where she named you mountain man of the month?" I say, giggling.

"Yes, and she's already hinted about Jonas being Mr. July."

"Come on. You are her nephews. Did you really think you were going to get out of this whole scheme untouched? I was surprised she didn't make you Mr. January."

He shoots me a glare that I know that there is no threat behind.

"Plus, with the success of the other guys, I doubt we'll ever be able to get her to stop now. Once she has all you mountain men matched up, Lord only knows who she's going to move on to."

"Well, I'll be the one that breaks her streak."

We order our lunch along with a piece of chocolate cake to share, just like we do at every one of these meetings.

"So, what are you wanting to do for this outing?" He asks after we place our food order.

"There's this Renaissance Fair a few towns over that the kids there have been talking about and are really wanting to go to. I've been researching it, and it's all outdoors with lots of vendors under tents. Though there are a few places that would be inside of a building, which are really just small little cabins."

Jensen listens to me and nods his head thoughtfully.

"That sounds like a good idea. The rest of the MC club is ready to help out. This is a mandatory event, so that will offer plenty of security, just in case."

Smiling gratefully at him, I say, "That would be

great. I think the kids will really enjoy it. Plus, it'll give them all a chance to have some fun and forget about their troubles for a little while. Also, it will give the moms a break from thinking of everything they still have left to do to get back on their feet."

While we ate our lunch and shared the chocolate cake, we continue discussing the details of the outing. Just like always, the conversation flows easily between us, and I find myself enjoying his company more than I should. But I try to push those thoughts aside.

As we finish our lunch, Jensen's hand brushes against mine when he reaches for the last bite of cake. My heart stutters in my chest at the contact.

Captivated, I watched him spoon the last bite of chocolate cake and then bring the fork to his mouth. His lips wrap around the fork and his tongue darts out to catch the last morsels of cake.

Knock it off, Courtney, I think to myself. Jensen is off-limits. But as we walk out of the cafe and towards our cars, I can feel Jensen's eyes on me. It's like he's trying to read my thoughts, and I can't help but feel exposed.

"Oh, don't forget about the hike you promised Landon for his birthday. His mom told me this morning. Apparently, that is all he's been talking about. He's really excited. Though I can tell she's nervous, but when I promised that I would go with you guys, that seemed to calm her down."

Landon and his mom have been in the shelter for a few months now. It was only just this week I was able to get her in for surgery to repair a bone in her arm that didn't heal right from the domestic abuse.

The improper healing of the broken bone wasn't allowing her full strength in her arm. Combine that with a very high-energy son and the need to be able to have a job to take care of him, it was a necessity.

Between her insurance with her now employer and what I could get the woman's shelter to help with, we were able to cover all of her surgery costs. The downside is we had to do the surgery this week, which also happened to be her son's birthday. When I asked him what he wanted to do for his birthday, thinking that maybe we could do something at the shelter, he said he wanted to go camping.

Overnight camping isn't really an option. But I was able to plan a hiking trip since Jensen and his twin brother Jonas own the outdoor camping store in Mustang Mountain. They also do a lot of guided hikes and know the woods around here better than anyone, well except maybe Hades the town's pet wolf. Though I don't think he'd make a good guide for a seven-year-old.

"I haven't forgotten. Yesterday, I went out on the trail I want to take him on to make sure that it was good to go, and also to clear anything that was in our way. Jonas is putting together a little hiking pack for him today and I will be there Saturday morning to pick you two up. Wear good walking shoes, jeans, and layers. As for you, better wear those hiking boots that I got you last year."

"I already have them set out," I say.

When he gives a small nod of approval with a smile, it makes my heart flutter.

"Good, I will see you on Saturday morning." He says, while opening the car door for me as I get in.

This is just Jensen. No matter what we do, he always walks me to my car and helps me in making sure I'm safe inside. I'm pretty sure it's some brother's code of 'hey, take care of her for me, will you?'

It's a standard I've come to measure other guys by. Though it is probably why I've had many failed dates since coming back home after college to Mustang Mountain.

Before heading off to college, Jonas and I broke up and went our separate ways, but we stayed friends. Back then I didn't even look twice at Jensen. But the four years away at school definitely changed him for the better and now I wonder how I missed him and ended up with Jonas instead. They are twin brothers, though not identical, but both are still good-looking.

On the drive back to the women's shelter, I try to focus on everything that I'm going to need for our hiking trip. It's great that both brothers are very successful with their outdoor store and their hiking trips. For sure, they know what they're doing. Even though I know Jensen will be more than prepared, I don't like ever being the damsel in distress either.

Once I'm home, I finish packing for the trip. I've got a camel water backpack, along with some trail mix, and have even got all of Landon's stuff organized and laid out, too. My hiking shoes that he helped me pick out last year are ready to go.

Part of me can't wait for this hike and getting to spend the day with Jensen even if we have Landon there. The other part of me dreads he will see I can't fit into a big part of his life and that will be the final nail in the coffin with us.

I should want that. But every time I try to push him away, I just draw him in more and more.

CHAPTER 3
COURTNEY

JENSEN HAS ONLY BEEN inside my place twice and the last time was over a year ago. We normally meet at the shelter or in town. He's driven me home plenty of times sure, but he hasn't stayed and come inside. Until now, he hasn't had a reason to enter my house.

As I pull my keys from my purse to unlock my door, a cool breeze fills the air, carrying the scent of wildflowers, pine trees, and rain from the forest outside. My mind races to make sure that I cleaned up this morning. There's no way that I want to be embarrassed about something lying around because I hadn't expected company. It'll be my luck that my vibrator is out for him to see the moment we walk in.

When I open the door, I take a quick glance and thankfully, I don't see anything glaring. But still having this man in my space is making me nervous. Although we've been friends for a while, spending time at each other's house hasn't been something that we do. Keeping him at an arm's distance makes it easier to be around him. That way, being in public, I'm more able to resist him than in the small confined space of my place or his cabin.

"Sorry about the mess. I wasn't planning on having company," I tell him. Then I set my purse down, and try to shove the mail scattered on the entry table into the drawer.

"I know you weren't and trust me, if you saw my cabin right now you wouldn't even worry. For weeks, I have laundry stacked and folded in several laundry bins that have not been put away. I'm pretty sure Jonas has left the pizza box on the kitchen counter instead of throwing it away. For several days he's been claiming that he's still going to eat that last piece," he says, shrugging out of his jacket and slipping off his shoes by the front door.

"Somehow, that doesn't surprise me. He never was the neatest person. Let me check and see what there is for dinner." Then I hurry into the kitchen because I am not wanting to talk about my ex.

"You know what? Why don't you let me cook dinner and you relax? I know hiking is exhausting, so I'm sure you're tired," he says, walking into the kitchen.

He isn't wrong. Hiking is his thing, not mine. I'm usually sitting behind the desk or helping out at the shelter. Plus, the idea of his making dinner intrigues me.

"Okay, let's see what you got," I say, sitting down at the kitchen island to watch him.

Jensen effortlessly moves around my kitchen, checking out what's in the refrigerator and in the pantry. After setting things on the counter, he pulls out pots and pans. There's a confidence in him that I didn't expect, especially in the kitchen.

When he starts chopping up vegetables with the skill of a trained chef, my curiosity gets the better of me.

"Where did you learn cutting skills like that?"

"Well, before Jonas and I went to live with Aunt Ruby, I grew up in that commune that's on the other side of the mountain. They taught us how to cook at a young age, so that we could help out. It was a big thing in the commune that everyone pitched in to help each other. It's stuck with me and is something that Aunt Ruby continued to teach me. I got to say, it's come in pretty handy." He smiles at me warmly, his eyes crinkling at the corners.

"Jonas never really talked about your time at the commune. I had no idea. He just said that you couldn't stay with your parents anymore, so your aunt Ruby and your uncle Orville took you two in. Because he never really wanted to get into the details, I never pushed it."

No one in town really talked about it. Now that I think about it, with Mustang Mountain being such a small town, you would think it would have come up at some point somewhere even as a passing comment.

"It's not really something that we talk about too much, especially back then."

Since talking about the commune seemed to make him uncomfortable and he shared something that I didn't know about him, I figured I'd tell him something about me.

"You know Jonas and I broke up because we went off to school. We went our separate ways. In college, I dated a guy and things went well. So well, that in my junior year we moved into an apartment together off campus. He was a football player and had a horrible, painful injury not too long after that. When he got heavily addicted to pain medication, it completely changed his personality." I stop and take a deep breath.

Jensen sets the knife down, leaning on the counter with his eyes glued to me, searching my face.

"Things got pretty bad. So I ended up at a woman's shelter to help me get back on my feet and still stay in school. Without the support of the amazing women there, I don't know what I would have done. It's what made me want to help others. So when I got the job at the women's shelter here, I knew it was time to pay it forward. It was never the job I had thought I'd be doing, but I absolutely love it."

When I had mentioned Jonas, the air between us grew heavy as if he had been brought into the room. We both knew our connection had started because of him, but our attraction has grown into something more profound. The intensity of the moment was palpable.

My heart is racing in my chest and the feeling of

Jonas being here with us is something we can't seem to shake. Neither of us mentions it as Jensen finishes cooking dinner.

Over dinner conversation is easy, like it always is between us. But once dinner is over things get awkward once again.

After dinner in an attempt to break the tension, Jensen asks me. "Hey, do you have a deck of cards? I'll teach you how to play this silly card game my mom taught me."

Immediately, I grab a deck of cards out of the end table in the living room. After a few rounds of the card game, which has no name and no actual set of rules, we're laughing and having a good time and back to our normal selves.

We continue to play the card game late into the night, each round punctuated by laughter and light-hearted banter. It felt as if we were old friends, effortlessly picking up where we'd left off, and I couldn't remember the last time I'd felt so at ease with someone.

Eventually, he catches me trying to hide a yawn.

"We should probably head to bed; it's been a long day," he says, standing to stretch and put the cards away.

I show him to the guest room, and we pause outside the door.

"I really appreciate you letting me stay here." Then, unexpectedly, he pulls me into a hug.

These hugs are familiar and normal between us, but this hug feels different. It lasts longer than normal.

So, when he finally lets me go, I look up at him and the heat in his eyes is undeniable.

As Jensen's eyes lock with mine, the air around us seems to crackle with electricity. My heart pounds wildly in my chest. I don't know who moves first, but we slowly close the distance between us. Our breaths start to mingle, and we hesitate for only a moment.

As if guided by some unseen force, our lips meet in a tender exploratory kiss. The sensation is like a thousand tiny fireworks going off inside of me, filling me with warmth and desire. His lips are soft and firm, gently coaxing mine open to deepen the kiss.

Gripping his shoulders, I need to steady myself against the intensity of emotions that threaten to sweep me away. His arms wrapped around my waist pull me closer to him. As I'm pressed up against his solid muscular body, my body wants more. The taste and feel of him and his intoxicating scent fill my senses. I want to enjoy this stolen moment forever.

When the notifications sound on his phone goes off, we're pulled back to reality, and he steps back to look at me. He has a dazed look on his face that I'm sure matches mine. Neither of us seems sure what to say as we stare at each other for a moment more.

"I'm going to head to bed. Goodnight Jensen," I say. Not wanting to hear how much of a mistake that kiss was, I turn and pretty much bolt to my room, closing the door behind me.

As I lie in bed, all night my thoughts raced, replaying the events from the evening over and over. I can still feel Jensen's lips on mine and just the thought of the kiss turns me on. No matter how hard I try, I can't shake that memory. The look in his eyes is one I know I will never forget.

But in spite of the undeniable attraction between us, we can't go there. I could see it in his eyes when we pulled away from that kiss as reality started to sink in. There's no way he would choose me over his brother, and there's no way I'd ever ask him to.

So, all we will ever have is this one stolen kiss after a long night of playing cards. I have to be okay with that.

In the darkness of my room that night, I made a silent promise to myself to not allow myself to venture down the road of 'what ifs.' That road will lead to nothing but heartbreak and prevent me from sometime later giving some great guy a chance.

Even though I know I don't have a shot in hell with Jensen, why the hell is he the only guy on my mind?

CHAPTER 4
JENSEN

AS I TRUDGE up the path to the cabin that I share with my twin brother, I can't help but replay yesterday's events. The hike with Landon, and then the evening with Courtney. Being stranded at her cabin felt more like a choice than a necessity.

Then there is that kiss. Holy shit, that was one hell of a kiss. There's a whirlwind of emotions inside of me. The undeniable chemistry between Courtney and me has grown stronger. Now it's to the point, it's hard to ignore. But her past with my brother complicates things. The worst part is I don't think there's anyone I can talk to about it.

As I step onto our front porch, I desperately try to push away the feelings from earlier. Opening the door, my pulse quickens and I see Jonas sitting by the fireplace. His brows are furrowed as he turns the pages of the book that he's reading. When I close the door behind me, he looks up at me and all the guilt of what happened last night comes rushing back.

"Hey man," I say softly, suddenly not sure if I want to stay or turn around and run to avoid any conversation.

"Where were you?" he asks, setting the book aside.

Freezing for just a moment, I've never once lied to my brother. While I know he won't mind that I took shelter at Courtney's house, but not telling him about the kiss feels like a lie of omission. Yet knowing the fact that it's never going to happen again, why bring it up?

"I was with Courtney. We took Landon on the hike. Even though the weather said that there was no rain in the forecast, by the time we got to the waterfall and had a little snack and some water, there were storm clouds in the distance. We rushed back to my truck and got down the mountain before it started pouring down rain. Once we got Landon to the shelter, I insisted on driving Courtney to her house. But it was just too bad for me to try to make it back up the mountain after that, so I stayed in her guest room for the night." I tried to say it like it was no big deal, as I hung my coat up and slipped my shoes off.

If I didn't know my brother as well as I do, I never would have caught the slight expression shift at the mention of staying at Courtney's. But it was so fleeting that I have to wonder if I saw it or if I was just projecting.

"Yeah, that rainstorm came out of nowhere. It was crazy. I wouldn't be surprised if there's a lot of debris blocking the hiking paths. We'll have to make sure we check them really well before we take people out. How is the hike with Landon otherwise?" he asks.

"It was good, and he loved it. When we turned the corner, Hades was standing in the middle of the path. But Landon handled it like a pro. It was a great teaching moment to instruct him what to do in case he comes across a wild wolf. Then Hades walked with us up to the waterfall, got something to drink, and we gave him a little snack. As the storm started to roll in, he took off. My guess towards Mack's to guard Persephone since she's pregnant with their pups."

"Yeah, that wouldn't surprise me either. You need to go get ready and clean up so that we can meet up with Courtney and take these kids to the Renaissance Fair."

"Yeah, Courtney was up really early. I think she's stressed out about the event, even if she won't admit it," I say.

Deciding to have a quick shower, I go to the bathroom. As the hot water cascades over me, I can't help but wonder if Jonas still has feelings for Courtney. When they both went off to different colleges at the end of their senior year of high school, they broke up amicably. I know that he's done. Hell, he's probably dated every single girl within a driving radius of Mustang Mountain, but still there's a lingering doubt in my mind.

We don't really talk about Courtney as his Ex. Really, she's just our contact at the women's shelter and my friend. They work together well when they have to, like at events that we'll be doing today. But I don't dare ask him about it because that's a can of worms I'd rather not open.

By the time I get dressed, I find Jonas outside with Jackson and Emma, Ford and Luna, and Ace and Shaw. I know the rest of the guys will join us at the meeting point. Since we decided to rent a commercial bus for the trip, everyone will be in one vehicle. It'll make it a lot easier for us to protect the kids both on the way there and on the way back.

There's an excited buzz in the air because even though we're there for protection, we're also there to enjoy ourselves. We get on our bikes and as the engines roar to life, this is what we live for. Helping others and making a difference in our community.

As we ride down the winding mountain road, a few of the other guys join us along the way. Finally, we get to the meeting spots where we always meet Courtney for these types of events. It's a clearing off the side of a road that isn't used and a place really only the locals know about. Though we do make it a point to change the meeting location from time to time just to be safe.

Courtney waves from the large front window of the bus, and we nod and head off. A few of the guys take the lead out front and the rest of us all ride behind the bus.

In front of me are Ford and Luna, and Mack and Lily. The girls are sitting in the back with their arms wrapped around their guys. I'd bet anything that underneath those helmets the men have huge smiles on their faces. I want that more than anything.

When we finally get to the Renaissance Fair, the excitement amongst the women and children is tangible. As the kids depart from the bus, their eyes are wide, and are full of excitement.

Approaching the entrance to the Renaissance Fair, we can feel the excitement amongst the kids grow. The scent of roasting meat and the sounds of lively music greet us. It's impossible not to smile as we take in the elaborate costumes, the knights in shining armor, and everything from fair maidens and flowing gowns to fairies covered in glitter.

Of course, my eyes land on Courtney. For a moment, I'm frozen in place. She's wearing a long flowing dress and her hair is done up in a style that pulls away from her face, but still lets her hair flow down her back. She looked stunning, and the kids gravitate towards her wanting her attention. I admire how she takes control of the situation.

Aunt Ruby and Uncle Orville greet us at the gate. They always like to support Jonas and me where they can, and it never hurts to have a few extra eyes when you have this many kids running around.

Once through the gates, everyone seems to form their own little groups. Courtney gravitates towards me with Landon, his mom, and a friend of his, who I'm assuming is the other kid's mom as well.

Strolling through the busy fairgrounds, we take in the colorful tents and stalls offering everything from handcrafted items to food. With all the colors and varieties, it catches your eye. One area is filled with the scent of freshly baked goods and spiced cider. After getting the kids a soft pretzel from a nearby vendor, we take in some juggling and fire breathing shows.

Even Jonas seems to be enjoying himself among his little group. At one of the shows, Courtney sits next to me. When Jonas looks over at me, I try to gauge his reaction. But if he has any thoughts, he keeps them close to his chest because they don't show on his face.

After the show, we get up and wander around some more and Uncle Orville comes over to join me.

"I can tell there's something on your mind. You want to talk?" He says as we hang back and let the group with Courtney's kids walk ahead of us.

"There is, but no offense, it's not something I want all over Mustang Mountain." I shoot a pointed glance at Aunt Ruby who's watching us from a nearby craft booth.

"She sure can gossip with the best of them," he chuckles, slapping his hand down on my shoulder. "But I learned a long time ago not to tell her everything. If you ever need to talk, I'm here for you and it can stay just between us." With that, he goes over and joins Ruby at the craft booth, where he pulls out his wallet to pay for the few items she already has in her hand.

I'm going to need to talk to someone about this, but my options are very limited. The guys in the club are going to have a sense of loyalty to not just me, but also Jonas. Especially the ones that grew up with us. If I talk to Aunt Ruby about it, it'll be all over town and that's the last thing I need.

Normally, I'd go and talk to Courtney, but she's the last person I can talk to about this. I can't go to my uncle because he can't keep a secret from my aunt, who is the biggest gossip in town. At the moment, the only person that it looks like I can talk to and not have it get back to my brother is Hades. Too bad that wolf can't give me advice, because I could sure as hell use it right now.

CHAPTER 5
COURTNEY

WITH THE RENAISSANCE Fair in full swing, I take a moment to just enjoy how happy everyone seems. Kids from the shelter are having the time of their life and have permanent smiles etched on their faces. They deserve this type of happiness after everything some of these kids have been through, and their moms too.

Watching Jensen interact with the kids in our group makes my attraction to him grow. He's so gentle and patient with them. It's such a contrast to the big muscled, tattooed biker guy that I'm beginning to understand why he's such a turn-on for women.

As we walk around with the group that Jonas is with, one of the little girls is drawn towards Jensen. Her name is Belle and back at the shelter, we like to call her Tinker Bell. She's normally pretty shy and all the people around seem to overwhelm her. At only four years old, she always carries around a plush baby doll that she calls Cuddles.

Right now, she's gripping that baby doll with one hand like her life depends on it. The other hand is wrapped around Jensen's leg, holding him close as we stand at a donut booth waiting for a turn.

"Would you like a chocolate doughnut?" he asks, bending down to eye level with Belle.

She nods shyly, and he swoops her up into his arms and lets her pick out the one with sprinkles that look like glitter. When he glanced over at her mom in a silent question of is it okay, her mom nods with a smile and a hesitant look on her face.

Right now, these moms are always worried about who their children will bond with because they're already dealing with so many people in and out of their lives on a regular basis. I also know from talking to them that many of them are worried about their kids having a skewed view of men because of what they've gone through.

Belle here is a prime example. She's scared of pretty much all men, so the fact that she's so comfortable around Jensen screams volumes. After we all have donuts, she holds Jensen's hand as we walk around and take in some of the sights. When we get to the face painting booth, her whole face lights up and she becomes completely animated in a way I have not seen.

Again, he glances at her mom silently asking permission. Her mom nods, and he helps Belle pick out a design. After they flipped through a few books, she eagerly points to a fairy that has wings.

"Oh, that's not only a good choice, but it's a special

choice. If you get this painted on, you're no longer just Belle. You become a fairy Belle," Jensen says.

"Like Tinker Bell?" the little girl asks.

"Exactly like Tinker Bell. It's a big step. Are you ready for that?" He asks in a mock serious tone, and she nods her head eagerly before jumping into the chair for the lady to paint her face.

The woman is absolutely wonderful with Belle. She asks about Cuddles and tells her the story of how a fairy was scared just like her. But when she would put on her fairy mask just like the face paint, she'd become brave, and do amazing things.

Once Belle has her face painted, we take some photos. Then as we step away from the booth, the scared little girl is gone and in her place is a confident little girl who can smile big.

"Games! Look at the games!" She squeals as we come up along a row of carnival games.

"Let's see if we can win you some prizes." They spend the next hour playing some games and Belle walks away with a necklace and a cute little stuffed wolf, which in my opinion, looks a lot like Hades.

Watching Jensen interact with Belle and the other kids only makes the attraction I feel towards him more powerful. He seems to know exactly what they want or need and always checks with their parents before doing anything. But his stepping in gives the moms a little chance to relax, which I'm sure is greatly needed.

All day long I watch how patient he is with them when they can't make up their mind and how protective he is of making sure they don't put themselves in dangerous situations. Four times that I can count today, I've had to remind myself that he's Jonas's brother and completely off limits.

"Hey, Courtney?" Someone calls my name and I turn to find Jonas and his group. Immediately, I go over to make sure everything's all right.

"Hey, what's up?" I ask, joining their group.

"The next jousting show starts in about thirty minutes, and I wanted to make sure we'd still be here because I promised the kids we could go," he says. When the kids hear his words, they start jumping in telling me about all the things that they can't wait to see at the joust.

While I'm talking, I feel eyes on me. Glancing around, I find Jensen watching me while Belle is playing some game with bean bags.

"Yeah, we should still be here. I don't think the kids are ready to leave just yet."

We talk for a few more minutes and I'm glad I've had a chance to see Jonas with the kids. He was never a kid person, but he's doing really well with them, which shows me he's grown quite a bit. But there's no denying the spark that was once there is long gone. I don't feel anywhere close to the way I feel around Jensen.

Once again, feeling Jensen's eyes on me, I glance his way and find him still watching. I feel a twinge of guilt for the growing attraction between Jensen and me, even if he is my ex's brother. But even from here, I can tell he shares the same feelings as I do, though we can never act on them.

Most of our group gathers at the joust and relaxes after what's been an already long day. The kids have a blast watching the entire performance, especially the parts with the king and the queen and the banter between the knights.

As the joust is wrapping up, one of the women near me goes pale and grips my arm.

"That's my ex," she whispers and nods to a man walking down the aisle beside us.

"We need to get them out of here. One of the women's exes is here and it could put everyone at risk." I lean over and tell Jensen.

Just like that, he and Jonas fly into action, word spreading quickly among the guys.

Immediately Jonas takes control of the situation, guiding both the woman and her two kids back to the bus. Then Jensen sends out a quick text to everyone and you can see phones start going off and the guys around the arena checking them. It's as if they've had this plan in place because everyone knows what they're doing. Not wanting to draw attention to us, each group slowly starts making their way out onto the bus.

"Alright guys, we need to head out. I know we had planned to stay a little bit longer. But it's very important that you all listen and don't draw any attention to us as we head back to the bus, okay?" Jensen says in a very grave but soft tone. The kids seem to understand that it's a serious situation, and no one makes a single complaint.

Once on the bus, Ruby is there with a clipboard in hand, checking off names as everyone gets on. Before getting on the bus, Belle stops and looks at Jensen and her eyes are so sad.

"Will I get to see you again?" She asks in her tiny little voice.

"You can bet on it. I work with Courtney all the time." He winks and ushers them onto the bus before turning and answering questions from anyone in line. He has this unflappable sense about him that calms down those who aren't quite sure what's going on.

With Jensen taking control, I'm almost not sure what to do other than to smile and assure everyone that everything's fine. Jensen's ability to handle the situation with so much care and patience and keep the children calm and even get a few of them to laugh during all this is making my heart do crazy things.

Once everyone is on the bus, I'm the last on board and I stop and stare at the Mustang Mountain riders all gathered around the bus. The few that are out on their bikes are ready to follow us and lead the way. My eyes lock with Jensen's for a brief moment. That spark that's always been there is stronger than ever and it's becoming harder and harder to deny my feelings for him.

Then Jonas steps up beside him and looks over at me with a nod and I swear it's the universe's way of reminding me that I can't go there. No matter how I spin it, Jonas still hangs over both of us. Neither one of us is going to hurt him, least of all Jensen. I nod their way and then turn to take my seat as the bus door is closed behind me.

As the bus pulls away from the fair surrounded by the guys and their girls on their bikes, I take a deep breath. I know when we get back to the shelter, there's going to be a ton of questions. Pulling up my phone, I start sending out some texts to let everyone there know that we were on our way and what to expect. Also, I ask one of the counselors to be available to talk to the woman who saw her ex and make sure that she's all right. Trying to keep busy with everything ahead, so I'm not thinking about Jensen. But unfortunately, the ride is just too long and before I know it, he's back on my mind.

My heart keeps trying to tell me that what is here is worth fighting for, that it's worth trying to overcome all the obstacles. Then my brain kicks in and says it's not worth hurting Jonas over, and it's not worth coming between two brothers either. Finally, I try to shake away the thoughts and turn to focus on the women and children on the bus with me.

The atmosphere on the bus is a mix of exhaustion and slight nervousness. Many of the children are leaning against their moms fast asleep. Their sweet faces still showing off the face painting and many still have smiles on their faces. On the other hand, many of the adults are staring out the window and I'm sure they have a lot on their mind.

The entire goal of this trip was to take their mind off of everything for a while and I think we accomplished that right up until the very end. Hopefully, it was enough of a reprieve and fun for the kids to have been successful. Only in the coming days will we be able to tell.

Once back at the shelter, the kids wake up, and everyone starts heading inside. Many of the children come up and give me a hug and thank me for taking them to the fair. Every one of the kids talks about how they had such a great time, most of them stating they've never been to the Renaissance Fair before, but can't wait to go back.

When I join them inside, the children are all gathered together telling stories about what they saw and did today. They talk about the things that their group watched, and the food that they tried. It's obvious that the little nap on the bus was exactly what they needed because they're a buzz and full of energy.

Despite how the day ended, I can't help but feel proud that I was able to give them this and how well it went off for the most part. I know Jensen and Jonas will be excited to know how happy the kids are and how they're already trying to plan to go back next year.

After everyone is settled, I gather my things and head home. Thankfully, there are some leftovers from the meal that Jensen made the other night. I could warm those up for dinner. Instead of having to cook something because now that the high of being at the festival with the kids has passed, exhaustion is starting to hit me pretty hard.

While the food's warming up, I go to my bedroom and change into my pajamas before gathering my food and sitting down at the table. My thoughts swirl around the events of the day, but always seem to come back to one person, Jensen, and my feelings for him.

I think maybe we've just been spending more time together than normal. We haven't had the break in between to let myself decompress and pretty much talk myself out of my feelings for him, so that's why they seem so much more intense.

Yes, that's exactly what I need. A few days away, put some space between us. He won't even think twice about it. After an event like today, he'll know I have plenty to do at the shelter. Then we can grab a coffee or something later next week and catch up.

Space is exactly what I need right now.

CHAPTER 6
JENSEN

I DECIDED to take a long way home and enjoy the beautiful weather that we've been having. On Mustang Mountain, all the flowers are in bloom and the greenery is back on the trees.

The day's events keep replaying in my mind, and no matter how hard I try, I can't seem to get Courtney's face out of my mind. Today I saw her in a completely new light. She's in her element helping these women and children, and everything about her lights up when she's around them.

When I walk into my cabin, I'm not surprised to find Jonas is not home yet. Which really doesn't surprise me, as he usually has evening plans. Hanging up my jacket, I notice the stuffed animal I won for Belle in my pocket. She trusted me to hold on to it and keep it safe for her, especially in all the chaos of having to get everyone back to the bus. I was so caught up in everything that was going on that I forgot to give it to her before the bus pulled away. The stuffed animal now feels like a symbol of something so much more. It's a connection to a life I didn't know I was missing.

I've been perfectly happy living in my cabin up here, and sharing it with my brother on the rare events he's home at the same time as I am. One of my simple pleasures is taking the time to enjoy the outdoors. I deal with people while hiking, but that's what I do. Though I never would have gone to the Renaissance Fair on my own, if it hadn't been for Courtney needing help.

But I know those are the type of events that Courtney loves to go to in her spare time and suddenly I'm wondering what's the next event she's planning. She's still on my mind, with her laughter, her smile, and the way she looked at me today. I can tell something shifted between us.

Just the thought of her has my heart pounding. I'm drawn to her like a moth to a flame. Before I know it, my jacket is back on, and the stuffed animal is clenched in my fists as I go out the door. Only this time, I'm getting into my truck. The sun has since set and the night sky is filled with stars. Every mile that I'm closer to Courtney's house, I can feel the electricity growing stronger in the air.

I don't want to think about how this moment can change everything. My heart starts racing as I pull into Courtney's driveway. There's a soft glow of light coming from the windows of her cabin, telling me she's home. Taking a deep breath, I climb the steps to her porch and then knock on the door.

A moment later she opens the door and stands in front of me in her barely there cotton PJ shorts and the almost see through tank top held up by the thinnest of spaghetti straps. Her hair is up in a messy bun and there is a slight flush on her cheeks. I swear she has never looked so beautiful. My breath catches in my throat and for a moment I can't speak.

"When I got home, I found Belle's wolf in my pocket. I forgot I had it, as, uh," I stop trying to regain my thoughts. Though I can't help it as my eyes roam over her body. "I thought you could give it to her tomorrow. You know, when you go in." God, that was worse than a teenage boy trying to talk to a supermodel.

Her eyes light up as she reaches for the stuffed animal. When her fingers brush against mine, electricity shoots through my body and my gaze is riveted on her. I couldn't turn away if I had tried. Judging by her soft gasp of breath, she feels the same thing I do from just the small little touch.

"Thank you," she whispers. Then her eyes search mine as if looking for an answer to a question that she hasn't asked.

While she may not have asked it, the 'what now' question is hanging there between us. We can both tell things have changed and with the silence between us, a thick tension builds in the air. It's a battle of wills to see who will break first, and it's me who breaks.

"Is there anything left between you and Jonas? I have to know, Courtney," I beg.

She just shakes her head, her eyes never leaving mine. "No, there hasn't been in a really long time."

"Good," is all I get out before closing the distance between us and pulling her into my arms.

When our lips meet in a searing, passionate kiss, it's like our souls are trying to reconnect. She melts against me as I close the door behind me and turn her, pressing her against it. Then I let my hands roam over her body and her thin clothing.

As our kiss deepens, I press my body against hers, feeling every curve of her body. For years, I have wanted to get my hands on her. It's as if we've been waiting for this moment our entire lives. The tension between us is thick, and I know I have to have her. Right here. Right now.

Breaking the kiss, I take a moment to breathe and take my time looking at her. Her eyes are glazed over with desire and her lips are swollen from our kiss. I've never seen anything so sexy. Trailing kisses down her neck, I nip at her skin as I go. She moans softly and it's all the encouragement I need to continue.

"Jensen," she moans my name, and it sends shivers down my spine. I lift her up, her legs wrapping around my waist as I carry her to the bedroom.

The room is dimly lit, the moonlight streaming in through the window. I lay her down on the bed, my eyes never leaving hers. Slowly, I crawl over to her, and let my hands roam over her body. Then I pull her tank top up, revealing her luscious breasts to my mouth. Taking one of her pink nipples into my mouth, I suck and nibble gently. She arches her back, pushing her breasts further into my mouth, and moans loudly.

As I move my mouth to her other breast, my hand travels down her body, slipping under the waistband of her shorts. She's already soaking wet, and I can't wait to feel her around me. When I slide my fingers into her panties, I circle her clit with my thumb. She's so responsive, whimpering and writhing beneath me.

Breaking away from her breasts, I kiss my way down her stomach to her shorts. They are another obstacle, so I push them down her legs and off the bed. She watches me hungrily, as I move my mouth lower and lower until I reach her clit. When I tease her with my tongue, she shudders beneath me.

Sliding two fingers into her, I thrust in and out. Then I curl them to hit the spot, which I know will drive her crazy. I continue to thrust my fingers in and out, pushing her closer and closer to the edge. She's so tight and wet I can feel every wave of her orgasm as it crashes through her body.

She screams my name as her orgasm rocks her body. I quickly stand up, removing my clothes and pulling on a condom, and rolling it on. Kneeling between her legs, I push inside her, inch by inch. I can't believe how good it feels to be inside her. How right it feels.

Continuing, I thrust slowly, building up my rhythm as she moans and clings to me.

I grab her hips, pushing deeper and faster. Sweat is dripping from my forehead, and I can feel my orgasm building inside me. Then I push her legs up, changing the angle and thrusting even deeper. She cries out as another orgasm pulses, making her walls clench around me.

I keep thrusting, pushing her higher and higher until I can't take it anymore and I let go, screaming her name as my orgasm rocks my body.

We lay there in silence. I'm still inside her as our breathing slowly returns to normal. Laying my head down on her chest, she wraps her arms around me, holding me close.

This is what I've been missing all these years, the connection with another person. This is more than just sex and I can tell she feels it, too. We lay tangled in each other's arms, and I can't help but think that this might be the beginning of something incredible.

In this moment, I feel a peace I've never felt before and know that no matter what happens, this is what I want in the end. And I also know I'm willing to fight for it.

Courtney's eyes flutter open, and she gazes up at me, her expression filled with wonder. Brushing a strand of hair from her face, I let my fingers linger on her cheek. No words need to be spoken because we just said it all with our bodies.

We lay there, wrapped in each other's embrace, as the first light of dawn starts to creep in through the window. The world outside is waking up, and with it, a new chapter in our lives begins.

Until it all crashes when my phone rings.

CHAPTER 7
COURTNEY

WE'VE SPENT most of the night making love and getting to know each other on another level. I feel safe and loved in his arms and savor the feeling. But the serenity of the moment is suddenly shattered by the shrill ring of a phone.

Jensen groggily reaches over to grab it, his voice thick with sleep as he answers. "Hello?"

I sat up to look at him and watch his face turn to stone-cold serious. Concern fills his handsome features, and I can tell something is very wrong.

"What happened?" he asks. Then listens as the person on the other end of the phone speaks, but I can't make out what they're saying. "I'll be there as soon as I can," he says. Then he hangs up the phone before jumping out of bed.

The urgency in his movements has me getting up to follow him worried that something happened to his brother or someone else we know.

"What's wrong?" I ask as I throw a shirt on and follow him to the bathroom.

"My dad got into a fight and has been flinging Buffalo chips at a stranger who he swears has been following him. He has all the signs of early dementia, but I can't convince him or my mom to get him into a healthcare facility. I need to call Jonas and get over there," he says, pulling on his jeans.

Even though we haven't talked much about his parents, I know that this is serious.

"Well, I'm going with you," I say, getting dressed.

"What no. Stay here. I know you need to get back to the shelter today anyway," he says, slipping his shirt on.

"This is what I'm trained in, Jensen. Deescalating a situation and besides, I did a turn at a dementia and Alzheimer's unit while I was in school."

I'm already getting dressed, but I notice his hesitation for just a moment before he nods his head and we both finish getting ready.

He helps me on his motorcycle and makes sure I'm on behind him before the engine roars to life beneath us.

"Hold on tight, babe," he says, pulling my arms around him so tight that my front is pasted to his back. As we race down the winding mountain roads, with the wind whipping through my hair, I hold onto Jensen tightly. His strong presence grounds me.

I've heard some talk of the commune outside of town. But I've never been there myself or even passed by it, so I have no idea what to expect as we get there.

As we pull into the commune, it's like stepping into another world. Everyone here is friendly, and they treat Jensen like family, even though I know he hasn't lived here in almost two decades. There are a couple of older women sitting in rocking chairs knitting and watching some of the people working in a small garden.

"Your dad is down by their place," a gentleman says after greeting us. It's obvious that Jensen is worried because he takes no time for introductions. Following him back through various small buildings, when we round one of the corners, there's a small crowd gathered.

Jensen charges right in. We find an older man, who I assume is his dad, still hurling Buffalo chips at a man on the other side of the circle of people.

"Hey, Dad, what's going on?" Jensen asks, stepping up beside an older woman. I can only assume it is his mom, judging by the way he pulls her into a hug and the look of concern and sadness on her face as she stares at the older man.

"This man here needs to go, but no one will listen to me. He's not a good person and he should not be here." Then he flings another Buffalo chip at him.

This is also the time Jonas walks up into the crowd and looks around at the situation.

"Who are you?" Jonas asks the man.

"I'm Lucious but you can call me Lou," the man says, pushing his glasses back up his nose. "We have things under control here, but thank you."

"Well, this is our dad, so we will take care of it. But maybe you should leave so we can get him to calm down," Jonas said.

But Lou was already shaking his head. "You just don't understand how things are done around here. We are a community and help each other. We don't need outsiders."

Jonas looks over at me and I can see how pissed off he already is.

"Help Jensen with your dad. I got this guy," I whisper to him.

He nods and walks over to his dad while I walk over to Lou.

"You're right. I am an outsider. Since they're busy, I have some questions," I say as soon as Lou's attention is off of Jensen and Jonas's dad. Fortunately, they seem to have calmed him down and they are helping him in to a tiny home behind the crowd.

"Well, I'm happy to talk to you before you leave. But only if you'll allow me to get cleaned up first," he says pointing to the stains all up and down his shirt and pants caused by their father.

"Of course," I say, stepping back. Then I nod and smile at a few of the other people as I head towards the building that the guys have disappeared into.

"Something just doesn't seem right about that man,"

Jonas says, putting words to exactly the gut feeling that I was having.

"I agree," I say.

"If you'll stay here and help Jensen, I'm going to go ask around about him. I've never seen him here before, and Jensen and I are here a couple times a month visiting."

"Of course, go, just be careful."

I stand back because Jensen seems to have everything under control, but when his dad sees me, his mood shifts.

"Which one of you boys brought this beautiful girl home? You couldn't give us a heads up so we could have prepared a meal and set out our finest linen for her?" He says in a very flirty voice.

"Dad, this is Courtney, Courtney, this is my mom and dad." Jensen introduces us.

"Oh, it's so good to finally meet you. We've heard so much about you from both our boys." His mom says, coming over to give me a big hug. Now the mood has shifted. It's much lighter and there are lots of smiles.

We sit and chit-chat about the women's shelter and the work that I've been doing until Jonas walks back in the door.

"It seems like everyone is singing this guy's praises, but his story changes based on who you're talking to," Jonas says with a sigh.

"I told you. He's lying to everyone, but no one believes me. It's obvious that he's got that smooth, slick car salesman attitude and could sell snake oil to the devil himself," his dad says. Then he gets up and goes into the kitchen.

The three of us step out onto the porch.

"Is there anything we can do to find out more about his background?" Jensen asks.

"Asher has a buddy at the police station. If this guy is giving us his real name, we can do a background check. But if he's up to no good, I doubt he'd be giving us his real name," Jensen says and we both agree.

Opening up my mouth to speak, I don't get a word out when we all hear commotion coming from behind their parent's house. When we walk over to see what's going on, we see Lou take off and bolt into the foothills just behind the commune. Without even thinking, the three of us take off after him.

"He's heading toward the creek," Jonas says, making it evident they know this land from growing up here.

My heart is pounding, and the adrenaline is racing through my veins. You don't run unless you have something to lose or something to hide. He looks back over his shoulder at us and then darts off the trail into the woods. I bring up the rear, letting the guys determine the path ahead of us because all the foliage is slowing me down a bit.

Jonas, on the other hand, seems to thrive in it and picks up speed before tackling Lou. Jensen is right there to help pin him down, and we all take a moment to catch our breath.

"You guys have no right to do this. I didn't do

anything wrong," Lou says as he struggles against our grip.

"Then why did you run?" Jonas asks, his voice stern.

"I didn't want to deal with you guys. You are outsiders," Lou spits out the word like it's poison.

"Jonas and Jensen are family here and I'm here to help them," I say, trying to diffuse the situation.

Lou looks at me with a sneer. "You're just a city girl. You don't know anything about life out here."

I bristle at his words because I am anything but. Though I don't get a chance to respond because Jonas cuts in, his voice low and dangerous.

"You don't know anything about us or what we're capable of. You better start talking now before things get ugly."

Lou's eyes widen for just a moment before his condescending attitude is back.

"What are you going to do? Run off and tell Mom and Dad? No one believes that crazy, old man anyway."

"Because you made sure they didn't," I say, putting the pieces together. Lou's expression shifts to one of surprise, and I can tell we've hit a nerve. He struggles against our grip once more, but we hold him firm.

"What are you talking about?" he asks. But his voice is now laced with fear, though he tries to hide it.

"You've been gaslighting the old man. Making him appear crazy so that no one would believe him when he tried to warn everyone about you," I say, anger seeping into my voice.

Lou's eyes dart around, and I can see him calculating his next move.

"But our dad wasn't crazy, was he? He isn't suffering from dementia. It's just lines you fed everyone. Want to let us in on your little plan?" Jensen says.

"These people here will believe anything if you give them something to gain out of it. They are the most easily manipulated group I've ever come across. If they think it benefits anyone else here, they will give you money. They have no idea of the real world. Come on, you got out of this place. You know this. I'll cut you in and we can all get rich," Lou says trying to change tactics.

"You're right. They are good people and my family. They don't need to know anything about the outside world, because that's what they have us for," Jensen says. Then he slams Lou into the ground, which causes Jonas to lose his grip. It's enough for Lou to be able to get up and run.

He runs deeper into the forest and my gut twists because we are getting further and further off the trail. Though I have to trust Jensen and Jonas to know how to get us back to the commune. I'm so lost in my thoughts, following Jensen that I don't realize he and Jonas have come to a stop and I crash into his back. Then there is a deafening roar echoing through the trees followed by Lou's screams.

When I try to step around Jensen, he stops me and turns, burying my face in his chest.

"Don't look. You don't want to see this," he says. While he holds my head to his chest to block it out, he and Jonas slowly start backing us up further into the woods.

"Cover your ears," Jonas says as he fires a gunshot in the air toward the bear.

"He ran off. But we should get out of here. There's no telling what the blood will draw in," Jonas says.

"Is he... is Lou..." I can't get the words out because my mind is spinning with all the possible scenarios of what they don't want me to see. It makes me wonder if my mind is worse than what is actually there.

"He's dead, and it's not pretty," Jonas says from beside me.

Turning my head so I can look at Jensen, his face says it all. There is no question Lou is dead. Otherwise, he'd be running to try to help him. It's a sobering reminder of the harshness of nature and the consequences of one's actions.

"Let's get her out of here," Jonas says, turning his back toward what is left of Lou. "You got her?" He asks Jensen.

"Yeah," he replies.

"Okay, I got your six," Jonas says.

We start walking, but the adrenaline that had been coursing through my veins is now fading, leaving me feeling cold and numb. The forest seems to stretch on forever, and I can't help but wonder if we've ventured this far into the woods during our pursuit. My legs feel like they're made of lead, each step taking more effort than the last.

As we continue our trek back to the commune, my breathing becomes shallow and my vision starts to blur. Panic wells up inside me, and I realize that I'm going into shock.

"Jensen," I manage to choke out, my voice barely a whisper.

"She's going into shock," Jensen says, but his voice sounds so far away.

Before I know it, Jensen is picking me up and carrying me through the woods.

"Just breathe, Courtney, we got you," he says as I rest my head on his shoulder.

I enjoy his comfort and try to block out the gruesome images that threaten to overwhelm me. With everything I see and work with on a regular basis, and with the women and the environments they come from, you would think this wouldn't faze me.

Maybe helping people out of a situation while they are alive is different from having the bad guy meet a horrific end. As we finally break free from the dense forest and the commune comes into view, relief washes over me. The familiar sight of the cabins and the people we care about is a balm to my frayed nerves.

They go right to their parent's cabin and Jensen sits on the couch with me on his lap. He wraps his arms around me, and I snuggle in as a warm blanket is placed over me.

People are talking around me, but I don't hear much of it. Instead, I soak up Jensen's warmth. I don't know how long I'm there and I must have dozed off. Because I wake up to the wonderful feeling of Jensen rubbing his hand up and down my back. His mom is sitting on the other end of the couch and his dad is in a chair beside the couch, but Jonas is nowhere in sight. That's when I start to realize what this position looks like between us.

"Mom made some food and there's some water on the coffee table for you," Jensen says in a soft voice as I wake up.

"Where is Jonas?" I ask, reaching for the water in front of me.

"The cops got here, so he took them out to where Lou was."

We stay and have lunch, chatting until Jonas comes back. When he steps in the door, his eyes go right to me sitting at the dining room table beside Jensen.

"You look a lot better. My mom's food always worked wonders for us growing up too," Jonah says before he comes over and gives his mom a kiss.

"I have to get going back to the shop, but I'll come in and check on you guys tomorrow to make sure everything is still going okay," Jonas says before turning to his dad.

"No more Buffalo chips. I don't even want to know where you got that many from." He says, giving his dad a hug before heading out.

Jensen allows me to finish my meal before he turns to me.

"We should head out to get you home. You need to get some rest," he says.

Even though I want to protest, I do feel exhausted.

"Thank you so much for helping us, Courtney. Why don't you go outside with me and let Jensen talk with his dad for a bit before you go," his mom says.

Then I follow her out to the front porch. Once the door closes behind us, she reaches into her pocket and pulls out a little satchel, and hands it to me.

"I want you to have this little token of our appreciation." She says, handing it to me.

"Oh, you don't have to do that."

"I know, but I think that this token is slightly selfish. A mother just wants her children to be happy."

Her words spike my interest, so I take the satchel and open it up to find some pink, white, purple, and red crystals.

"Anyone with eyes can see how happy you and Jensen make each other. I know your history with Jonas, so I hope this will help you through that journey. The pink one is a rose quartz and is known as the love stone. It will help you sort out your feelings for the boys and help you love yourself. This white one is a moonstone that is great at bringing couples together. But if you're also having trouble sleeping from all this, place it is under your pillow. This purple one is an amethyst, and it should help bring you mental clarity on the path that you should take. Now, this red one is a carnelian, and it's great for supporting relationships and helping to build a healthy sex life." She winks at me, but I can feel my face turning as red as the carnelian stone she was just talking about.

Then a thought flashes through my mind. If everyone else picked up on what's happening between Jensen and me, does that mean Jonas did too?

CHAPTER 8
JENSEN

MY MIND RACES the entire way to Courtney's house because of the conversation that we're going to need to have once we get there. Even though I know she's tired, I think it's best to get things in the open.

Once we get to her place, I help her off the bike. "Can I come in? I think we need to have a chat," I say while she hesitates for a moment.

Following her inside, I sit down next to her on the couch. I swear she knows what I'm going to say before I say it just by the look on her face.

"Last night was amazing and everything I have been dreaming of. But us crossing that line was a mistake. I can't hurt Jonas like that and my loyalty to the club won't allow it. Jonas has been the one person in my life that has been there through everything, and I can't lose him. The look you gave me when he saw you asleep on my lap..." I trail off, unable to finish the sentence as I see the hurt written plain as day on her face.

She places a hand on my knee and tries to force a smile.

"I get it. I do. I'm not saying I like it, but I get it and won't hold it against you. But I don't want to lose the friendship that we've had."

"I don't want to lose it either."

"Good. Now I'm going to go to sleep for several days and you need to go find your brother," she says.

As I go out to my bike, her words leave me feeling dismissed. Once on my bike, I go straight home thinking maybe I could catch Jonas before he leaves to go to the shop. Not wanting to let this fester, I need to face it head on. Whatever anger he might have towards me, I want to address so it doesn't ruin our relationship.

But he isn't at the cabin. Looking around, it doesn't look like he's been there recently. My anxiety starts to grow as I head into town and to the shop, hoping to find him there. Only the shop is closed and also doesn't look like there's been anyone there at all today. His truck wasn't at the house and it is nowhere on the street either. So in a last-ditch effort, I go to the Mustang Mountain Riders clubhouse hoping maybe I'll find him there.

As I enter the club, I find Jonas sitting at the bar and he doesn't even look up to see who's walked in. I sat down next to him, feeling the eyes of the other club members on us, but staying back and giving us space. When Jonas just takes a swig from his drinking and glares at me, I know I've messed up. Then I brace myself for his lashing out.

"You know, I'm not even mad that you and Courtney are together. I thought for a few years now that you two would make a great couple. You work well together and you seem to get along, but I wasn't going to push the option because the last thing I want is for someone to push me into a relationship." He says with not even a hint of anger in his voice. But his tone is flat.

"But I expected if something was happening, you'd come to me and tell me. You're my brother. Why would you keep something like this from me?" He finally turns to look at me.

"You're my brother and she's your ex, so I always saw her as off limits. To me, it didn't matter what my feelings for her were. For a long time, I suppressed my feelings for her. But then the night I got caught in the rain and stayed at her house, being in her space was almost too much. We kissed, and I stopped it because of you. Nothing happened until last night. Then we got the call to go to the commune. It's a shit excuse but..."

"Yeah, it is. If you had feelings for her, you could have come to me and talked to me."

"I didn't know if you had feelings for her and the last thing I wanted to do was hurt you."

"Well, I don't have feelings for her which you would have found out if you had talked to me. What hurt me was my own brother lying to me and keeping this from me and finding out the way I did."

Now I'm feeling desperate to make things right, no matter what it takes. I believe that if he does forgive me, it will help me feel like I've paid for my mistake. At the very least, it might make him feel better.

"Go on, Jonas," I say, trying to provoke him. "Hit me. You know you want to. If it was anyone else, you would."

But he just shakes his head and takes another sip of his drink. He's grown a lot over the years and doesn't want to resort to violence. He's not the same impulsive kid I grew up with.

But I know my twin better than he knows himself sometimes, and I can see it in his face. He wants to hit me, but he's holding himself back. So, I start pushing a few of his buttons.

"Well good. It's not like you're capable of a serious relationship anyway," I slap his shoulder and stand up. Yeah, I can see the moment he snaps.

But I don't get any warning other than the moment I saw him crack. The next thing I know his fist connects with my jaw, sending me stumbling back a few feet.

The force of the blow surprises me. Jonas really has grown up since the last time we fought. He's no longer the brother who was learning how to fight. The one that I would protect and who would always be protecting me. He stands up and this time I see it coming, but I don't try to move or stop it. When his fist hits, it connects with my temple.

"That second one is for egging me on after I said no," he says.

A searing pain radiates through my head and at that moment, time seems to stand still as if the universe itself is holding its breath to see what our next moves will be. Then I watch a barrage of emotions flutter across his face: anger, betrayal, and finally one of regret. In the next blink of an eye, everybody sprints into action.

Arms wrap around me, pulling me back. At the same time, Jackson and Miles get in front of Jonas, keeping him apart from me. The throbbing pain intensifies, and my hand instinctively rises to cradle my temple.

Jonas's eyes meet mine. But judging by the murderous look Jackson is giving us, I know I have to deal with more than just my brother. Now I have to settle this with the club.

CHAPTER 9
COURTNEY

PACING AROUND MY LIVING ROOM, I think about everything that just happened. Even with the thoughts racing through my head, I was still able to get a little nap on the couch. But the moment my eyes popped open, Jensen was on my mind again and it hadn't stopped.

While I know how I feel about him, I also know I can't be what comes between him and his brother. Yet I know deep in my heart that I can't continue just being Jensen's friend. Not anymore. That thought alone kills me.

Finally, I go into the kitchen to grab a glass of water or anything for a distraction, but no sooner do I sit down at the kitchen island with my water than my phone goes off. Right away, I'm racing back into the living room, hoping it's Jensen.

I'm disappointed when I see that it's not him. Then I give myself an internal kick because while it may not be Jensen, it is Lucy. Not only is she my assistant at the woman's shelter, she's also the one person who knows how I feel about Jensen and everything that's been going on. Outside of Jensen, she's my closest friend.

"Hello?" Instantly, I'm worried that something's happened at the shelter.

"Courtney, are we friends?" she asks.

I'm taken aback by the question because it's nowhere close to where I thought this conversation was about to go.

"Of course we are."

"Then why do I find out that you and Jensen are together because I overhear some people talking about it at the café?"

I collapse onto the couch. People are already talking about me and Jensen? This is really not good.

"How the heck did people find out?" I say more to myself than to her.

"You forget how small of a town this is. Asher called his friend down at the police station, which got people buzzing about what was going on down at the commune. When he got back, he had to fill everyone in. Of course, Donna's sister was the receptionist there at the police station, so she called Donna first thing, who was just finishing up her shift at the Mustang refuge. Then, Donna not wanting to get scooped on the gossip called Ruby straight away. Now Ruby has been claiming to anyone who will listen in the café that they're getting together is another matchmaking win for her Mountain Men of the Month."

After her recital of the gossip, I decide to not beat around the bush. I jumped right into what happened at the commune, down to Jensen taking care of me and Jonas putting two and two together and Jensen bringing me home and racing off after his brother.

"Wow, it's like a real-life fairy tale and everything," she sighs dreamily.

"The problem is I don't know what to do."

"From everything that I know about you and Jonas, you and he just went your separate ways. There was no bad blood, and you weren't each other soul mates. Neither of you is pining for the other, so it shouldn't be a big deal. Other than the fact that neither of you told him and he found out the way that he did, which to be honest, was kind of shitty."

"I know," I say because it completely was. Though I keep telling myself that there really was no time to go and talk to him because everything happened so fast. But in reality, I've had feelings for him for a long time and I could have talked to Jonas at any point.

"Honestly, everyone that knows the two of you knows that you're perfect for each other. I have been really rooting for the two of you to get together. Now that I know that you have, I'm going to tell you not to let anything get in your way. Stop pacing around your house overthinking like I know that you are and go after him. Stand up to Jonas if you have to because his brother doesn't get to dictate your future or Jensen's. But I know Jonas and I guarantee you he's just going to want both of you happy."

We hang up, and I pace the living room for a little while longer before I realize that she was right. Jonas has always wanted Jensen to be happy and me too. He's tried to set me up on a few dates that only proved he just had no idea what my type is. But in a tiny town like Mustang Mountain, you don't turn down a date.

Going into the bathroom, I brush my hair, pop on a little lip gloss and mascara, and change my clothes before I head out. I'm not going to let him push me away. I'm going to do everything that I can, so at least I know where I stand. If I have to close the door on this part of my life, then so be it. But I'll do so knowing that I did everything I could.

I go straight to Jensen's cabin figuring that's where he and Jonas would probably have this out, but neither of their cars is there. Next I drive into town checking at the cafe and even drive by Ruby's house. Nothing. With a last-ditch effort, I go by the MC clubhouse, where I find not just their trucks but many of the other members as well.

A pang of nervousness hits me. I've never been inside the club, never been invited in, and I know if I were to just knock and ask to see Jensen, they would turn me away. Not knowing where this burst of competence comes from, I just walk through the front door as if I've been there a million times.

The entryway opens to a big open area with a bar on one side. Sitting on one bar stool is Jensen, with a steak on his eye. A few stools down Jonas is laughing and talking with some of the other guys with ice on his knuckles.

It doesn't take a genius to put two and two together and realize that these brothers had it out physically rather than verbally. But the moment I step into the room, they all stop and look at me. I think everyone's stunned that I had the balls to walk in uninvited.

Taking a deep breath, I pray that my self-confidence and determination hold as I walk over to Jensen.

"You know that's a waste of a perfectly good steak. You could have at least used a bag of peas that no one would have cared about throwing away," I say, walking up to him.

The whole room bursts into laughter at my words. "Oh, after he's done with it, we're grilling it up and making him eat it. Don't you worry, sweetheart," one of the older members, whose name I don't know says.

Surprise is written all over Jensen's face. Without a doubt in my mind, he did not expect me to show up, here of all places. Glancing over at Jonas, I see the same surprise on his face as well.

"Courtney..." Jensen says, lowering the steak from his eye.

There's a purple bruise forming, and my heart hurts seeing him like this.

"If you think I'm going down without a fight, you're wrong," I tell him.

When I turn back to Jonas, he has a huge smile on his face. "I didn't like the way that I found out, and I wish you guys could come and talked to me sooner. But

I'm not stopping you and I'm not going to get in your way because pretty much everyone in town knows the two you are meant to be together. Just warning you, I better not be the last to find out other important news about you two. Whether it's about your wedding, babies, or whatever the future brings. I better be the first to know."

Without thinking, I walk over and wrap him in a big hug.

Jonas wraps one arm around my waist with the ice still in his other hand. "But make sure you make him work for it," he whispers in my ear.

When I look back at him, he winks, and had a smile that lit up his face.

Turning to look at Jensen, I could see his eyes were darting between me and his brother. The twins seemed to be having some sort of silent conversation. Though I can't read the expression on Jensen's face and I'm not sure I would like to know what was there if I could.

But when he takes a deep breath and stands up, setting the steak down on the plate at the bar, I definitely don't like the look on his face. My heart sinks at the words I know are about to come out of his mouth.

CHAPTER 10
JENSEN

AFTER MY BROTHER and I calmed down, the guys got me the steak for my face and a bag of ice for Jonas's hand. Then we had a heart-to-heart in front of all the guys and I laid all my cards out on the table. It was just pure dumb luck that Courtney happened to walk in when she did. Though it was perfect timing.

Now that she stands there in front of me, I am nothing but a bundle of nerves. But there's no chickening out now. So as I stand up, I keep my eyes on her because I'm terrified I'm making the wrong move, but this is something that I have to do.

One last look at Jonas shows he has a beaming smile on his face.

Walking over to Courtney, I drop to one knee in front of her. "Courtney, I have loved you for longer than I think either one of us is willing to admit. You're the first person I want to see when I wake up in the morning and the last person I want to see before I close my eyes at the end of every day. I'm tired of beating around the bush and denying my feelings for you. I love you." Then I reach into my pocket and pull out the ring that the girls helped me make in yarn from a twisty tie.

"Will you marry me?" I ask, holding the ring up.

When she sees it, she laughs, and I can see the love in her eyes. But then instantly a wall goes up and she turns to look at Jonas, who still has a smile on his face. He nods as if answering the question yes. Jensen and I have already talked about this and he's okay with it.

She turns back to me, the wall is long gone, and her eyes are shimmering with tears.

"Yes!" she says.

I slide the temporary ring on her finger. "This ring is only temporary. I made it because I planned to go talk to you tonight and ask you to marry me. We'll get you a proper ring this weekend." I tell her as the cheers go up all around the room.

People started coming up to us offering congratulations and welcoming her to the family. As things die down, I take her hand and pull her toward the door.

"We need to go talk to Aunt Ruby before the news reaches her. Otherwise, if we don't, we will never live it down."

She hops in my truck, and I know her car will be safe here until we come back to get it. It's one of those rare days where Aunt Ruby is not at the mercantile, but actually at home. Before we even get a chance to knock on the door, she meets us on the porch.

"Did I forget a meeting? You know the other day I forgot to pencil in a doctor's appointment. If they hadn't called, I would have missed it. I've just been so busy. The tourism website has to be rebuilt with all the traffic it's been getting, and the cabins are booked out a year in advance. Can you believe it? So, forgive me if I forgot our meeting, please refresh my mind on what we're meeting about," Aunt Ruby finishes breathlessly. Then she gives me a hug and turns to hug Courtney.

"No meeting and you didn't know we were coming. We wanted to make sure that you heard from us the latest Mustang Mountain gossip," I tell her.

Her face lights up with a smile. "Oh, come in, come in, let me get you some huckleberry tea, and these new biscuits I've been looking to try out to sell at the mercantile. You can give me your opinion while we're at it.

She starts fluttering all around, gathering up the biscuits and making the tea. Only once she is sitting down with us, does she finally turns back to us.

"Okay, what is this gossip that you have for me? And you know I don't condone gossiping." She gives me a pointed look, as if she's not the biggest gossip in town.

Looking over at Courtney, I take her hand in mine and smile at her. She looks back at Ruby and holds out her hand.

"We're engaged!" she says.

I expect Aunt Ruby to be excited and joyous, but

she just stares at the ring as if it's the most hideous thing she's ever seen.

"What in blazes is that thing?" She says her eyes are still on the ring on Courtney's hand.

"It's just temporary. I didn't have time to go get her ring, but I'll fix that this weekend.

Without another word, she stands up and leaves the room. Courtney and I just stare at each other not sure what to do.

"Well, I love this ring." She leans forward and gives me a kiss. I'm about to get up and leave when Ruby walks back into the room.

"This was my mother's ring. I decided a long time ago that whichever one of you boys got married first, I was going to give it to you. If Jonas ever settles down, I have one for him too." She hands me the beautiful antique ring that is absolutely stunning. I don't remember seeing it before.

It's a large diamond in a beautiful floral setting. That she's giving me this ring to give to Courtney means the world to me.

"Well, what are you waiting for, boy? Propose properly to the woman. She deserves it," Aunt Ruby orders.

Obeying Aunt Ruby, I get down on one knee in front of Courtney who is sitting on the couch. Then I repeat my earlier words.

"Courtney, I have loved you for longer than I think either one of us is willing to admit. You're the first person I want to see when I wake up in the morning and the last person I want to see before I close my eyes at the end of every day. I'm tired of beating around the bush and denying my feelings for you. I love you. Will you marry me?"

"I love you too, Jensen. Yes, I will marry you," she says much softer this time, as I slide the ring onto her finger and pull her in for a kiss.

We stay talking with Ruby for a while and then decide to go back to her place. She hasn't stopped smiling and her beautiful moss green eyes are shining with happiness. When we step outside, two of the rubies on the ring catch the sunlight and they sparkle brilliantly. Something in the back of my mind says to capture this moment because it seems important even if it is just appears to be an ordinary instant in time.

When we arrive back to the MC clubhouse to get Courtney's vehicle, there are even more cars there now and they're blocking her in. Once we get inside, we found that the guys were throwing a big party for us. They're grilling food and have even broken out the best booze to celebrate.

"I thought we'd have a quiet night back at your place. But how does a party at the club here sound?"

"It sounds like the perfect way to celebrate our engagement," she says, smiling at me as we enter the clubhouse.

Seeing how easily she fits into my life, I'm not sure why I waited so long for this. But I'm damn sure glad we got here.

EPILOGUE
JONAS

THE CHORUS of Toby Keith's "I Love This Bar" drew me in as I pulled open the door to Ace's Place, my favorite watering hole in Mustang Mountain. I did love this bar. Loved that no matter what the hell was going on in my personal life, I could disappear inside and forget about it for a little while. Loved the cracked leather bar seats and the scent of beer that had seeped into the floorboards over the decades.

It was the kind of place where everyone knew your name, but no one bothered you unless you looked like you wanted company. I also loved that it was dim enough inside to hide how rundown the old building was, but the dozens of neon beer signs provided just the right amount of light for me to do a quick survey of the interior and make sure my latest ex was nowhere in sight.

I wouldn't say she'd been stalking me, but she kept showing up in the places I usually frequented. Since my Aunt Ruby had been handpicking mountain men from Mustang Mountain to plug as eligible bachelors, my ex had it in her head that I'd be in the hot seat soon.

If Ruby thought making part of her man of the month club would get me to settle down, she'd be disappointed. In my twenty-eight years, I hadn't managed to date a woman for longer than a month or two. As far as I was concerned, there was no reason to start changing things now.

"The usual?" Ace tossed a paper coaster onto the bar in front of me. Even though he was one of my Mustang Mountain Riders MC brothers, we didn't know each other that well. He'd only been in town for a couple of years.

When his uncle died, we all thought Ace's Place would close its doors forever. Thank fuck the old man willed the bar to its namesake, and Ace ended up sticking around.

I nodded, my throat parched and ready for an ice-cold beer. "A couple of the other guys should be here in a few. Put the first round on me."

"You got it." Ace set a tall mug of beer on the bar. "Were you out on a call?"

"Yeah." I took a swig of the beer. Damn, it tasted good. "One of the outbuildings at the old lumber mill caught fire. Chief thinks it was probably kids."

"You catch 'em?" he asked.

I grinned and shook my head. "Nah. There are too many places around there to hide."

Unlike Ace, I'd grown up in Mustang Mountain

and was probably more familiar than most about the best places to lie low when avoiding trouble. My twin brother Jensen and I had gotten into our fair share of trouble when we were kids.

Now that we'd grown into mostly law-abiding citizens, we were paying back our past transgressions by doing good deeds through the Mustang Mountain Riders MC and keeping an eye on the area.

"It's a good thing you guys were there to clean up their mess." Ace nodded, then turned toward a couple of old ranchers who sat at the other end of the bar.

I couldn't blame kids for being kids, not when I knew what it was like to grow up with a giant chip on my shoulder that never seemed to budge. But as a volunteer firefighter, I'd learned a hell of a lot about what could go wrong if a prank got out of control. Next time I came across the group of kids I suspected had been involved, they were going to get a few unsolicited words of warning.

While I waited for the other guys who'd been with me at the fire to trickle in, I glanced at my phone. There was a text from Laci wondering if I wanted to get together for a drink this weekend.

No.

And a text from Aunt Ruby asking if I was available for dinner on Sunday.

Yes.

The last message was from Jensen, asking me to give him a call as soon as possible. Even though our relationship had been a little strained lately since he'd taken up with my high school ex, he was still my brother. Anyone could see the two of them belonged together, and they both deserved to be happy.

Jensen and I might look the same, but that was where our similarities ended. He was the smart one, the funny one, the loyal one, the one who could be counted on in time of a crisis. As for me, well, I was always up for grabbing a beer with the guys or heading out for a good time. But when it came to the important stuff—the life and death stuff—Jensen was the Pike brother people wanted on their side.

He picked up without even saying hello. "Jonas. Where the hell have you been?"

"On a call. Some kids set fire to one of the buildings at the old mill. What's up?" It couldn't be something with Aunt Ruby or Uncle Orville. If there'd been an emergency, he would have said so on his text or just given me a call.

"I'm with Courtney at the women's shelter. We're trying to figure out a solution for one of the women here and could use a favor."

"Just say the word, bro." Jensen knew I was all-in with helping at the shelter. All the guys at the MC were. Oftentimes, we offered security for the women and kids who were leaving a bad situation or needed protection to get back and forth from court cases.

"It's not one of our normal requests."

"What do you mean?" I took another sip of my beer, wishing he'd just get to the point. I'd already put in a full day at the shop we ran together, then another couple of hours on the call. I was tired, and the smell of singed pine still clung to my skin, despite the long shower I'd taken at the fire station.

"It's a big ask, but remember, you owe me. And it's going to be a win-win," Jensen said. Something was off. I could tell by the undercurrent of nerves in his tone.

"What do you mean, I owe you? Last time I checked, you're the one who owes me. Didn't I come down the mountain last month and haul your ass out of the ditch?" It didn't really matter who owed who, Jensen knew no matter what might be going down between us, I'd always have his back just like he'd have mine.

"Yeah, but I wouldn't have gone into the ditch if you'd changed out the tires on the truck like you said you were going to."

He had a point, and I was too tired to argue. "Doesn't matter. Just tell me what I have to do."

"It's not for me, it's a woman at the shelter. Her name's Madeline and she's in trouble. Are you in?"

"Like you have to ask? What does Madeline need?" I didn't know why he was making such a big deal about doing a woman at the shelter a favor. The guys at the MC pitched in all the time. "Does she need somebody to go pick up the rest of her shit at home?"

Jensen cleared his throat. "Uh, it's a little more complicated than that."

"Why are you being cagey as fuck?" He was getting on my nerves. "Just tell me."

"Yeah, okay. Remember, you already said yes."

I practically growled into the phone. "Spit it out before I hang up on you, bro."

"Fine. She needs you to marry her."

WANT MORE JENSEN AND COURTNEY? **Sign up for our newsletter** and get the free bonus scene here: https://www.matchofthemonthbooks.com/JensenBonus

Make sure to grab Jonas's story in **July is for Jonas**. Then Ace is up in **August is for Ace!**

https://www.matchofthemonthbooks.com/July-Jonas

https://www.matchofthemonthbooks.com/AceAugust

MOUNTAIN MEN OF MUSTANG MOUNTAIN

Welcome to Mustang Mountain where love runs as wild as the free-spirited horses who roam the hillsides. Framed by rivers, lakes, and breathtaking mountains, it's also the place the Mountain Men of Mustang Mountain call home. They might be rugged and reclusive, but they'll risk their hearts for the curvy girls they love.

To learn more about the Mountain Men of Mustang Mountain, visit our website (https://www.matchofthemonthbooks.com/) join our newsletter here (http://subscribepage.io/MatchOfTheMonth) or follow our Patreon for extra bonus content here (https://www.patreon.com/MatchOfTheMonth)

January is for Jackson - https://www.matchofthemonthbooks.com/January-Jackson

February is for Ford - https://www.matchofthemonthbooks.com/February-Ford

March is for Miles - https://www.matchofthemonthbooks.com/March-Miles

April is for Asher - https://www.matchofthemonthbooks.com/April-Asher

May is for Mack - https://www.matchofthemonthbooks.com/May-Mack

June is for Jensen - https://www.matchofthemonthbooks.com/June-Jensen

July is for Jonas - https://www.matchofthemonthbooks.com/July-Jonas

August is for Ace - https://www.matchofthemonthbooks.com/AceAugust

ACKNOWLEDGMENTS

A huge, heartfelt thanks goes to everyone who's supported us in our writing, especially our HUSSIES of Mountain Men of Mustang Mountain patrons:

Jackie Ziegler

And to our Kickstarter supporter **Stephanie Scarim** for providing the inspiration for Lou's demise.

To learn more about the Mountain Men of Mustang Mountain on Patreon, visit us here: https://www.patreon.com/MatchOfTheMonth

OTHER BOOKS BY KACI ROSE

Oakside Military Heroes Series

Saving Noah – Lexi and Noah

Saving Easton – Easton and Paisley

Saving Teddy – Teddy and Mia

Saving Levi – Levi and Mandy

Saving Gavin – Gavin and Lauren

Saving Logan – Logan and Faith

Saving Ethan – Bri and Ethan

Saving Zane — Zane

Mountain Men of Whiskey River

Take Me To The River – Axel and Emelie

Take Me To The Cabin – Phoenix and Jenna

Take Me To The Lake – Cash and Hope

Taken by The Mountain Man - Cole and Jana

Take Me To The Mountain – Bennett and Willow

Take Me To The Edge – Storm

Mountain Men of Mustang Mountain

February is for Ford – Ford and Luna

April is for Asher – Asher and Jenna
June is for Jensen - Jensen and Courtney

Club Red – Short Stories
Daddy's Dare – Knox and Summer
Sold to my Ex's Dad - Evan and Jana
Jingling His Bells – Zion and Emma

Club Red: Chicago
Elusive Dom

Chasing the Sun Duet
Sunrise – Kade and Lin
Sunset – Jasper and Brynn

Rock Stars of Nashville
She's Still The One – Dallas and Austin

Standalone Books
Texting Titan - Denver and Avery
Accidental Sugar Daddy – Owen and Ellie
Stay With Me Now – David and Ivy
Midnight Rose - Ruby and Orlando
Committed Cowboy – Whiskey Run Cowboys
Stalking His Obsession - Dakota and Grant

Falling in Love on Route 66 - Weston and Rory

Billionaire's Marigold - Mari and Dalton

A Baby for Her Best Friend – Nick and Summer

CONNECT WITH KACI ROSE

Website
Facebook
Kaci Rose Reader's Facebook Group
TikTok
Instagram
Twitter
Goodreads
Book Bub
Join Kaci Rose's VIP List (Newsletter)

ABOUT KACI ROSE

Kaci Rose writes steamy contemporary romance mostly set in small towns. She grew up in Florida but longs for the mountains over the beach.

She is a mom to 5 kids, a dog who is scared of his own shadow, and a puppy who's actively destroying her house.

She also writes steamy cowboy romance as Kaci M. Rose.

PLEASE LEAVE A REVIEW!

I love to hear from my readers! Please **head over to your favorite store and leave a review** of what you thought of this book!

Made in the USA
Columbia, SC
23 September 2024